THE EGG TRAIL

Claudine M. Bigelow

Illustrations by Jonathan Liu

Primix Publishing
11620 Wilshire Blvd
Suite 900, West Wilshire Center, Los Angeles, CA, 90025
www.primixpublishing.com
Phone: 1-800-538-5788

Published by Primix Publishing: 06/14/2024

ISBN: 979-8-89194-118-2(sc)
ISBN: 979-8-89194-119-9(e)

Julie, who never doubted things are reachable;

John, who always questioned outer space;

Jan, who is with God and his angels;

Dennis and his constant inquisitive mind;

Darcy, who knows about rainbows;

Misty, who asked the whys and wheres for this story.

THE EGG TRAIL

In a small town lived a family. Zoey stayed home with her dad when her mom worked the evening shift.

One evening Zoey became sick. She was uncomfortable and did not want to be left alone.

"Daddy, Daddy, stay with me. Tell me a story, please, Daddy!"

"O.K., Zoey, but you have to stay in bed. Curl up in your blanket," her dad replied. "Well, now, what story should I tell you? ... Oh, I'll tell you the story about baby rabbits and chicks."

"Oh, Daddy, I know about rabbits and chicks."

"The ones from outer space?" he asked.

"No, I hadn't heard that one," Zoey responded.

Well, far from Jupiter and Mars lingers a planet called Zandar.

If you look really hard you can see it through the misty skies, nestled among the stars. The countryside is scattered with flowers. The shrubs are sprinkled here and there.

The sun kisses the dew off the greenery, preparing each blade of grass for the day.

Zoey, on Zandar chicks do not lay eggs. They plant seedlings. The seedlings grow into trees, with leaves the color of the rainbow. At adulthood, the trees are filled with eggs. As the days go by, each egg is enriched by the sun, becoming hard-boiled. Planet Zandar is the only place in the universe that has an egg orchard.

The bunnies take care of the orchard. They do this after school is out. Bunnies must keep up on their multiplication tables. They eat a lunch of rabbit pellets, carrots and—for dessert—a little lettuce.

They pick up their baskets to go gather eggs in the orchard. Each bunny is to gather two baskets full of eggs. The eggs are then laid aside for the egg-eating creatures.

When the chores are done, the Zandar bunnies can frolic in the sun. They can burrow in their holes, or relax and nibble on some grass.

One year the chicks planted too many seedlings.

The bunnies worked hard to keep up the orchard. It was no use. There were too many eggs, and they were spoiling. They smelled worse than dirty old socks. The smell was getting into the bunnies' fur. The bunnies dug a very, very deep hole in one area of Zandar. In the hole they buried the stinky eggs.

Zandar's law was not to waste or litter. The abundance of eggs was quite a problem.

There was only one thing to do: call an emergency meeting. The final decision came from two top council members.

The first council member was Mr. Tubby Tubbs, the bullfrog. The second was Mistress Anita Owl. They were the final word!

It was decided to travel through the solar system, giving to others. But … to whom? And where?

All agreed that Mars was out; it had less gravity. Jupiter is cold, and has frozen gases. Mercury, closest to the sun, is much too hot. Saturn has too many rings circling around it. These planets would not work.

Tubby Tubbs and Anita Owl had no answer.

"Mmmmm … My mind is waterlogged," said Tubby Tubbs in his low deep voice, his words sounding as if they were coming from the depths of his stomach.

"My head feels like it's still settling from jet lag. Let us take a moment of thought," suggested Anita Owl.

"Maybe we should meet in the morning!" Tubby Tubbs replied.

Rippytip Rabbit, the youngest member, spoke up. "Permission to speak to council?" he asked in a quivering voice.

"Permission granted, Rippytip," answered Tubby Tubbs. Rippytip sucked in a deep breath and slowly let it out.

"Sir, council members, I would like to suggest ... Earth!" Everyone looked at each other; they smiled. They all shook their heads and smiled again. Everyone was delighted.

"Of course! Earth has children," Anita Owl spoke out.

"We must pick out four unique bunnies and two chicks," Tubby Tubbs decided. The council agreed.

Among the four bunnies chosen to go on the trip was the inquisitive Poof. Poof got his name because he could appear ... then disappear. Poof was good at math.

The second bunny was Wobbelhurst. He usually spoke in single sentences which made you think. He had a sense of humor, and would tackle any situation.

The third bunny was Garby, a geographical whiz. His chortling laugh could echo throughout the countryside.

The last bunny was Tarbor. He was a big brown bunny, a quick thinker in a crisis. He had an unusual ability to sometimes blow a wind storm in another direction.

The first chick was Celty. She could look at anything and most accurately know its distance.

Last to be picked was Penelope. She was a small chick, but held an abundance of strength within her small frame.

Each bunny and chick was to carry two baskets of eggs.

"Please beware of falling stars; sometimes they do not stay in orbit," reminded Tubby Tubbs.

"We will remember," said Garby.

The group started out at dawn. The trip was very long.

The heat in the atmosphere was another concern for the group. They had to protect the eggs.

Penelope and Tarbor paired off. Excitedly they darted in and out of the clouds and stars.

Wobbelhurst saw Penelope and Tarbor. "Hey, stay strict with our mission!" he yelled out to them.

"Oh, O.K.!" Tarbor shouted back.

They all settled in for their journey. They were excited, happy, and somewhat fearful of what was ahead. They became more attentive to their trip.

A short distance into their trip, a gust of wind came up. The group felt something gently falling on them.

"What is falling on us from above?" Celty asked.

"Oh, FAB-A-DAB!" exclaimed Garby. "It's sand particles. Protect the eggs!" The group became quiet, looking all around. They had fallen into a meteor shower.

The wind began to rise; it continued in an almost forceful anger. It separated Wobbelhurst, Poof and Celty from the rest of the group.

Tarbor, Penelope and Garby found shelter behind a floating star. The star was not in the meteor shower's path.

Tarbor called out, as he blew at the winds. "Lost part of the team, call out your names so we know who is here."

Poof, Celty and Wobbelhurst did not answer. They had fallen onto a meteor.

Suddenly the wind tossed Penelope. She clung on, still holding her basket of eggs. Tarbor reached for her. He blew at the wind with all the strength he could gather. The wind did not move.

Again he reached for Penelope. Penelope relaxed her body like a limp piece of spaghetti. Tarbor pulled her up. She smiled, still holding her baskets.

"I tried blowing the wind away to help us. It is a good thing you relaxed," Tarbor said.

"It is O.K., Tarbor." They started laughing, relieving the tension. Garby chortled in laughter too. His laughter echoed throughout the solar system. Tarbor found he had more respect for Penelope and her quick thinking.

Wobbelhurst and his partners were still on the meteor. They felt luck was on their side, as they traveled toward Earth.

"Poof, Celty, are you O.K.?" Wobbelhurst asked, seeing concern on their faces.

Poof and Celty were clutching their baskets very tightly. "I feel like my fur has disappeared," Poof replied.

"I'm so scared I think my yellow feathers are turning white!" Celty squeaked. She then looked up, seeing something in the distance. "Hey, Earth is not too far," she remarked to the others.

"The wind can make you feel that way, Poof," Wobbelhurst explained. "Celty, how do you do that? Are we almost there?"

The winds of the meteor shower were slowing down.

"Oh, look, here come the others! And they are riding on a rock!" Garby said.

Suddenly the sky started clearing, and the group fell through a rainbow.

The meteor shower had dotted some of the eggs with meteor sand. The other eggs had a mixture of odd colors; some of the eggs were colored by the rainbow.

"Oh, FAB-A-DAB! Do you think the eggs are acceptable?" Garby asked the others. "They are not natural-looking."

"Well, my friend, it is too late now. We are arriving on Earth," Wobbelhurst chimed in.

In Kansas, a farmer tilling his field spotted Tarbor. He saw Tarbor's big eyes and a bundle of fur coming at him. The farmer yelled to his wife.

"Call NASA! Call the sheriff! We're being invaded … invaders are here!"

The bunnies and chicks started laughing. They decided to make the egg delivery to each town and state a game.

Each paired group went to their selected states on Earth.

That Sunday happened to be Easter on Earth.

On the Oregon coast, a dog spotted a green and yellow egg. He wasn't sure what it was, so he pawed it to destruction, and then ate it.

A cat played with an egg for fifteen minutes in a California backyard. A little girl laughed at the sight.

In Arizona, a snake slithered across an egg. He turned and pounced on it. He swallowed it whole.

A man on a Texas golf course mistook an egg for a golf ball. He teed off, and got a hole in one, winning his game. He had a surprised look on his face as he pulled a purple egg from the hole.

A little old lady in Iowa saw something in the grass. Thinking the egg was a mouse, she immediately beat it with her cane. Then, with a nod of her head, she straightened her hat and proudly walked away.

Other than these few funny incidents, Earth moms and dads thought it was a nice way to celebrate Easter.

As for Zandar, there are not always rainbows to travel through. The seedling crops are sometimes short, and there are fewer eggs. Once in a while there are storms, and the Zandar group cannot travel the solar system during these times.

The fun of egg hunts continues on Earth as moms and dads buy eggs. They hard-boil them. The moms and dads, and sometimes the children, dye the eggs together.

This way they help the Zandar creatures from outer space, who just wanted to share.

The Zandar saying:

Love is not put there to stay.

Love in your heart is loving when you give it away.

It is the giving and sharing that helps pave the way...

"Oh, Daddy! That's a great story. So that's why we have eggs at Easter?" Zoey smiled.

"Yep, sure thing, little one! Do you think you can get some sleep now?"

"Yes, Daddy. 'Night, Daddy ... Wait ... Wait ... Next year will I see bunnies at Easter?"

"It is a sure thing they will be somewhere. And the chicks, too, I'll bet. 'Night."

"Mmmmm ... 'night, Daddy ... awww ..."

END

ACKNOWLEDGMENTS

I would like to express my appreciation and thanks to the following for their help in research for this book:

Dr. Dugget via Mrs. Black of the US Naval Observatory (Almanac office), for travel time between planets;

Dr. Bob Harrington, for information on meteor showers;

Mr. Gruber of the OMSI Library, for information on light years;

Dr. Donald McCoy of the North Portland Animal Clinic, for information about the practice of dyeing bunnies and chicks with food coloring from the 1950s to the 1970s, a practice that was stopped due to the cruelty to the animals;

The Humane Society via Barb Bogarosh, Mr. Thomas and Mr. Olney of the National SPCA Archives;

Last but not least Gina Brewer, for her help with proofreading and editing.

ABOUT THE AUTHOR

Claudine Bigelow was born in Glendale, California. She was raised on the road along with three brothers and a sister. Her parents were magicians, and they lived in a world of show business. This adventure started when Claudine was four, continuing until she was twelve. Their mother schooled the children on the road.

Claudine has been doing artwork and writing since age ten. She is the mother of six. She took a two-year course pursuing her writing while her children were teens. She washed dishes for twenty-three years while raising her children.

She always curiously questioned things. Her childlike thinking and down-to-earthiness have helped her to survive the rocky parts throughout her life.

In the early seventies, her writing surpassed her artwork.

In 1986, Claudine published a How-To, three short stories for a leather magazine. She also published three poems in the International Library of Poetry (2000, 2002, 2003).

ABOUT THE ARTIST

Jonathan Liu has been drawing ever since he could hold a crayon. He doodles incessantly and reads a great deal. He's currently a stay-at-home dad in Portland, Oregon, where he is gaining notoriety for his Etch-a-Sketch artwork. Some of the results of his creativity can be seen at his website, www.RainyBayArt.com.